Has Anybody
Lost a Glove?

Has Anybody Lost a Glove?

by G. Francis Johnson

Illustrated by
Dimitrea Tokunbo

Boyds Mills Press

The illustrator would like to give special thanks to Indigo Washington,
Raina Washington, Sybelle Washington, Emily Carpenter,
Mercy Carpenter and Shannon Stalter.

Text copyright © 2004 by G. Francis Johnson
Illustrations copyright © 2004 by Dimitrea Tokunbo

Published by Boyds Mills Press, Inc.
A Highlights Company
815 Church Street
Honesdale, Pennsylvania 18431
Printed in China

Library of Congress Cataloging-in-Publication Data

Johnson, G. Francis.
Has anybody lost a glove? / by G. Francis Johnson ;
illustrated by Dimitrea Tokunbo.— 1st ed.
p.   cm.
Summary: Jabari sets out to find the person who has lost the blue glove
he finds when he and his mother leave the subway.
ISBN 1-59078-041-8 (alk. paper)
[1. Gloves—Fiction. 2. Lost and found possessions—Fiction.]
I. Tokunbo, Dimitrea, ill. II. Title.
PZ7+
[E]—dc22

2003026868

First edition, 2004
The text of this book is set in 14-point Stone Serif.
The illustrations are done in watercolor.

Visit our Web site at www.boydsmillspress.com

10 9 8 7 6 5 4 3 2 1

To my sons, Audley and Christopher. You are my inspiration.

— G. F. J.

To my friends Jody Magillicutty and Kent Brown

— D. T.

THERE IT LAY ON THE STEPS leading out of the subway. An almost new, navy blue glove. Jabari bent down and picked it up.

"I wonder who this glove belongs to," he said to his mother. "Can we find out?"

"Do you know how many people pass through this train station?" Mother asked as she pointed to the crowd of people. "That glove could belong to anyone."

"Please, Mom. How would you feel if it was your glove?" Jabari asked. Mother looked down at him and smiled.

"I guess I wouldn't be happy. You can try to find the owner . . . but it won't be easy."

Jabari and his mother left the subway station and
headed home. They walked past a noisy construction
site. Some of the workers were on their break.

Jabari saw frosty white clouds escape their lips as they laughed and joked with each other. Jabari walked over to the crew.

"Has anybody lost a glove?" he asked. The workers looked at the glove in Jabari's hand.

"It isn't my glove," said the foreman.

"Mine, either," said the crane operator as he climbed back on his rig.

"Besides," said another, reaching for his jackhammer, "we wear big, suede work gloves to do our jobs."

"I see," Jabari said, looking down at the glove. It's too small and soft for a construction worker, he thought.

Jabari and his mother continued down the street until they reached Li's Fish Market.

"Hello, Mrs. Wells. Hello, Jabari," said Mr. Li.

"Did you lose a glove, Mr. Li?" asked Jabari. Mr. Li looked at the glove.

"My gloves are made of rubber to keep my hands dry," said Mr. Li. He brushed aside ice to reveal a row of shiny fish.

"Oh," said Jabari. He looked at the glove. It wasn't made of rubber. Nobody's hand would stay dry in this, he thought.

Mother and Jabari met Matt, the delivery boy, loading his bike with a large pizza. The cheesy smell made Jabari's mouth water.

"Did you lose a glove, Matt?" asked Jabari.

"Not me," said Matt. "I wear these sports gloves. The strap looks cool, and they help me grip the handlebars on my bike."

"Oh," said Jabari. The glove he found didn't have a strap.

Mother took Jabari by the hand. They crossed the
busy street, directed by the traffic officer.

"Did you lose a glove today, ma'am?" Jabari asked.
The officer glanced at the glove.

"Why, no," she said. "My gloves are white so folks
can see my hands."

She held up one hand to stop the cars. With the other

hand, she waved people across the street.

"Hmmm," said Jabari. "No one would see her hand in a navy blue glove."

The glove didn't belong to a construction worker or Matt. It didn't belong to Mr. Li or the traffic lady. Who *did* lose this glove? Jabari wondered.

Jabari and Mother met their neighbor Mrs. Bigelow as she was leaving the beauty parlor. Her black, shiny hair smelled like sweet coconuts.

"Hello, young man," Mrs. Bigelow said to Jabari. "How are you?"

"I'm fine, ma'am. Have you lost a glove today?" he asked.

Mrs. Bigelow looked down at the glove. She puffed herself up and wrinkled her nose.

"Heavens, no. I wear only fine leather gloves," she said as she smoothed them with her hands.

"Aw, shucks," said Jabari. The tag inside the glove read 100% wool.

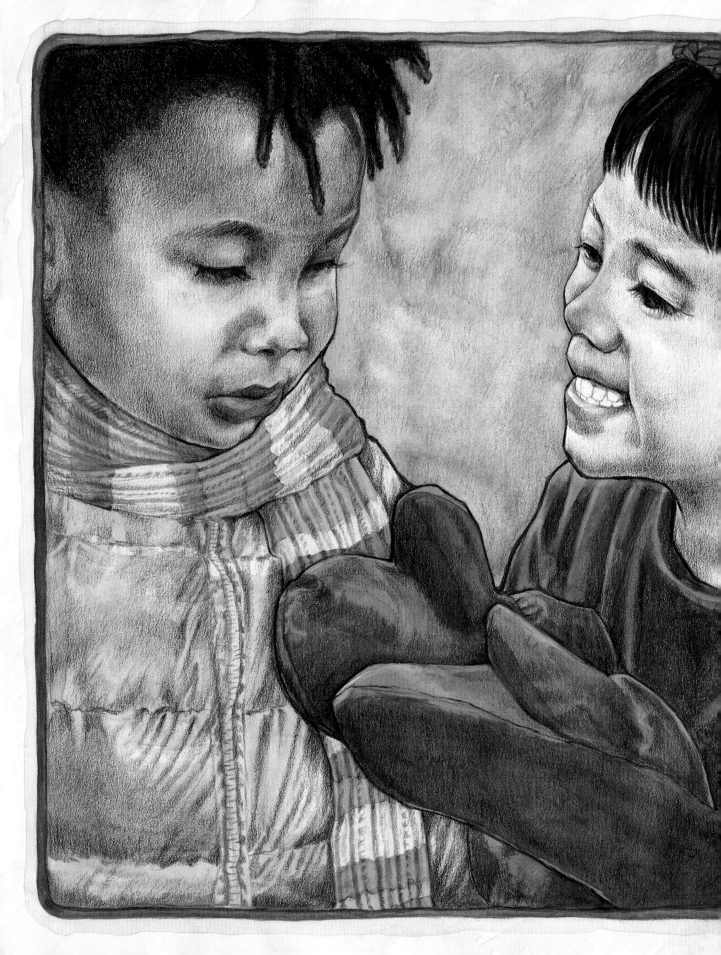

Mother noticed her son's troubled face. She patted him on the shoulder.

"I said it might be hard, honey."

Jabari perked up when he saw his friend Alex going to the laundromat. I bet this glove belongs to him, he thought.

"Hi, Alex," Jabari said. "Did you lose a glove today?"

"Nope. I wear mittens. They keep my hands nice and cozy."

"Ahh," said Jabari as he looked at the mittens. They were all one piece except for a thumb.

Rat-a-tat-tat. Tum-tum-tum. Jabari and Mother
followed the sound of the drum. Three teenagers sat
on wooden crates playing plastic buckets. A small
group of people looked on. Jabari pushed his way to
the front. When they finished playing, one of the
drummers stepped out from behind his drums.

"Have you lost a glove?" Jabari asked him.

"Not me," he said as he picked up a hat filled with money from the audience.

"Me, neither," said another packing up his drum. "Anyway, when we play the drums, we wear gloves with no fingers."

"Don't your hands get cold?" Jabari asked.

"Only when we stop," said the young man, with a wink and a smile.

The glove didn't belong to Mrs. Bigelow, or Alex, or the drummers.

"I wonder if I'll ever find who lost this glove," Jabari said to his mother.

"I told you it wouldn't be easy, dear."

Jabari was nearly home. He worried that he wouldn't find the owner of the glove in time. Just when he was about to give up hope, he saw a woman talking to a little girl. They stood on the steps of a brownstone. Jabari could hear the woman speaking as he got closer.

"Did you put it in your pocket, Crystal?" asked the woman. "I can't afford to keep buying new ones." The girl's eyes glistened with tears.

"I'm sorry, Mommy," she said, looking down at her shoes.

Jabari noticed that her right hand was bare. But on her left hand she wore a blue woolen glove. He looked at the glove in his hand. It was blue. It was woolen. And it matched his right hand.

"I think this is it," he said to himself. Jabari climbed the steps to the girl and her mother.

"Have you lost a glove today?" he asked as he held it out to the girl.

"Yes, thank you," said Crystal. "Look, Mommy, I got my glove back!" She took the glove and waved it in the air.

"My goodness," said Crystal's mother. "How did you find us?"

"Well," said Jabari, smiling, "it wasn't easy."